The Icelandic Yule Lads:
Mayhem at the North Pole

Written by

Heidi Herman

Illustrated by

Colleen Stiles

with contributions by Jessica Krumlauf

First Edition.

Hekla Publishing
ISBN-13 978-1-947233-88-1

This Book Belongs to:

____

Other Books by Heidi Herman:

Legend of the Icelandic Yule Lads
Yule Lads & Other Legends Coloring Book (with bonus short stories)
The Guardians of Iceland and other Icelandic Folk Tales

Co-Authored by Heidi Herman and Ieda Jonasdottir Herman
Homestyle Icelandic Cooking for American Kitchens

The Icelandic Yule Lads:
Mayhem at the North Pole

1

"I got troll trouble!"

Gully Gawk smirked as he heard the farmer's loud grumble. The man must have found the tipped-over and emptied milk buckets. Even the ones Gully Gawk left upright were drained dry to the last drop. He snickered as he jumped from hummock to lava rock, to where his brother Sheep Cote Clod hid.

Sheep Cote Clod loved fresh sheep's milk but his troll brother Gully Gawk preferred cow's milk. They loved to play tricks on the farmers whose herds they chased. Coming down from the mountains they would slink across the fields and around the edge of the barn to drink all the milk. They were quick and sly, and never caught. It was even more fun to chase the heard and get a fresh mugful during the day while the herds were in the pasture.

This day was just one of those. As Gully Gawk started to jump over the last rock, the earth shook and rumbled. The ground roll under them and Sheep Cote Clod fell backwards off his rock while Gully Gawk slipped and went face-first into the moss.

"GGGGRRRRR" they troll-growled in unison. That troublesome Katla volcano shook the earth and now she threatened to blow!

2

In the troll cave, four Yule Lads grabbed at stuff that went skidding and flying around from the earthquake. Suddenly, one troll with an abnormally large nose stopped and stared at the ceiling, his eyes glazed over and head cocked as if listening to a far-away melody of beautiful music.

It was Door Sniffer. He turned his head this way and that, his huge nose quivering as he inhaled deeply. Mmmmm – sweetbread and cookies. His eyes grew wide. From the smell of it, a very large amount. Tons! Heaps! Masses! A Plethora! He smacked his troll-lips and drooled in anticipation.

His troll brothers knew that look on his face. Pot Licker, Stufur and Spoon Licker were sure to follow where-ever that talented nose would lead.

As everyone knew, the best treats were homemade and the process created great piles of dirty bowls, pots and pans, and spoons galore. They had to reach them before some industrious person washed them. The great gooey globs and sticky stuff scrubbed clean from spoons and washed down the drain! Pot Licker, Spoon Licker and Stufur looked at each other in horror – they must find this wonderful kitchen.

"Uh, oh," Door Sniffer said as he ran outside, "I smell something else – grab the *Galdur Pokan*."

3

They ran through the night, with the green and purple ribbons of color from the northern lights racing above them. The night had a strange glow but the Lads were used to it and didn't even notice. Door Sniffer stopped now and then, popping into a guesthouse or sneaking through the deserted kitchen of a local hotel.

He sniffed carefully at each table. Nope, not the wonderful prize he was sniffing for. But, at each stop, they swiped snacks from tables and shelves, knocking over cookie jars and canisters, spilling dishes and generally leaving a terrible mess behind.

Running and giggling, they stuffed their faces with goodies as they ran, not paying attention to their direction until a sudden rumbling shook the earth under their feet. A huge crack opened up and the three went tumbling down.

"Get your foot off my face you oaf," Stufur cried.

"You get your elbow out of my ear," Spoon Licker yelled back.

Their shrill troll shrieks echoed, the sound bouncing off of the cave walls, making the ruckus they raised sound like ten times the trolls they were.

They all went silent when they heard they sound no one ever wanted to hear. They knew exactly where they were and it wasn't good. The one sound that could make a troll's scaly skin hairs stand on end - a rattle, followed by a slithering sound and a terrifying hisssss…..

Stufur scrambled to back up, hearing Door Sniffer behind him. They had fallen into the caves around Lake Lagarfljot. There was no doubt the Monster Worm was fast approaching. This was no ordinary little worm, this was a wingless dragon, a direct descendent of one of the Guardians of Iceland, and he was very powerful. He was a fierce protector of good and the Yule Lads, being trolls, were not going to be welcomed! Worse yet, they were half-troll, half-ogre, and the Monster Worm did not want them in his homecave.

Stufur crawled to Door Sniffer's side. To his great relief, Door Sniffer held tight to the Galdur Pokan, the Yule Lad bag of magic. Each had runes carved to identify the magic, but otherwise, they all looked a bit like rocks.

"Use it brother," he hissed, trying to be a quiet as possible.

Door Sniffer was fumbling with the bag, but it was dark. "Wait! I don't know what this is…" he whispered urgently to Stufur, who tried to grab the spell from his hand.

It was too late. The Monster Worm was in the cave and his massive foot-talon has grabbed ahold of Spoon Licker's ankle just as he tried to scuttle away! The cave lit up with the red ember breath that escaped from the Monster Worm's snout. Stufur, terrified, threw the spell and the cave exploded in a shower of sparks and a rainbow of colors.

"Oh, no, not *that* one," Door Sniffer cried and with a flying leap, jumped out of the opening they had fallen from and disappeared.

5

Stufur arrived at the Yule Lad cave, gasping for breath from his run.

Door Slammer saw his Stufur's wild eyes and ran after him, knowing instantly this was an adventure he surely didn't want to miss! He stopped short and stared as Skyr Gobbler and Sausage Swiper headed toward him, returning to their home cave after their most recent escapade.

Door Slammer did a double-take before he remembered they were in disguise! They looked so silly trying to imitate how humans looked, but they had to in order to blend in at the Taste of Iceland Celebration in the United States. Giddy, giggly and still stuffed from their trip to Seattle, they were all about joining in on another adventure. They switched paths and caught up with Door Slammer.

"What is wrong with Stufur?" they shouted as they rushed up.

"He looked like the Trollwife Gilitrutt was after him again!"

"Nay," replied Door Slammer, "I think he may have riled up the Monster Worm again and had a hand in that flood."

A dark shadow suddenly appear from overhead. It rushed over the ground, eating up the sunshine and quickly overtaking the trio.

Skyr Gobbler looked up and shouted, "Oh No - The Monster Worm and Gilitrutt together would have been better than this." Stubby stared and his eyes grew big as saucers….. "Uh oh……run!

Whew! That was a close one. The human's drone had unexpected flown over and very nearly got a full photo of all of them together. There was no troll magic that could un-do that evidence. They should learn from the pictures of the Monster Worm. Because of those, Loftur could only come out at night or on very foggy days. But it served him right, keeping Spoon Licker like that.

Skyr Gobbler shuddered as he thought about a life where he couldn't run from place to place – it didn't sound like any fun at all! Sky Gobbler looked across the cave they had ducked into to escape the drone's camera. Door Slammer and Stufur leaned against the wall watching Pot Scraper as he cocked his head, listening for the drone to leave.

"I need to talked to Sina," Stufur announced as he started to pace around the small enclosure.

"Sina?" Skyr Gobbler raised his eyebrows in surprise.

"Why do you need to consult with the Hidden Folk?" demanded Door Slammer.

"Well, um, ugh," Stufur sighed heavily, "we must help Spoon Licker, we need to save him."

Door Slammer narrowed his eyes. "What did you two do?"

Stufur stopped pacing and spun to face Door Slammer, puffing up his chest preparing his defense. "It was Door Sniffer….we followed him and..and…I barely got out. Door Sniffer went East – I think he's in Finland. But Spoon Licker is trapped. We must save him."

7

"It was not my fault." Stufur cried. "Door Sniffer said he smelled something wonderful… that huge nose of his was actually *quivering*." Stufur shook his head, "He said it was sweetbread and cookies! From the smell of it, a very large amount. Tons! Heaps! Masses! A Plethora!"

"What is a plethora?" asked Sausage Swiper, wrinkling his nose.

Stufur shrugged, "I don't know, but it sounded like it might taste good".

"How did that get Spoon Licker in trouble?" Door Slammer said, eyeing the door to their treasure room, itching to slam it shut.

"To save time, we'll go through the pass," Door Slammer said firmly.

Skyr Gobbler's eyes grew wide as saucers, "The *Pass*?"

"Uh, uh, no way. I love my brother but you're talking crazy." shouted Sausage Swiper.

"We have to use the pass, and you all know what we have to do to make it though."

"Oh, troll up, brothers!" Door Slammer shouted his encouragement at his brothers. "You are half-ogre trolls that have feared throughout Iceland for centuries. You can do this!"

"Yeah," Stufur chimed in, "Let's give 'em some *Troll Trouble*"

And so they did.

Sneaking and slinking, with a little hopping and one big leap, they worked their way toward the Monster Worm's cavern. They came to the Pass, home of Gryla, a hideous, evil, mean old crone. She was ancient and had terrified Iceland for generations.

The Yule Lads knew her as Mother.

If they made it though there, the other end was home to an old trollwife who was still angry her sister had been driven crazy by church bells and died years before falling off a cliff. But first, Gryla.

Part troll and ogre, she was also a powerful Seið witch. She used to be able to change her appearance whenever she wanted, but the Lads had stolen her magic spindle. But that is another story for another time.

They entered the pass running as fast as their troll legs would take them. They heard a screech and a furious yowl. It was mom, all right. Rocks pelted them and the earth shook in a sudden quake.

Skyr Gobbler ducked as Door Slammer threw a spell over his head. It landed with a thunderous roar then they heard a crash and the sound of water.

"Whee!" Skyr Gobbler crowed, "I think you brought part of the glacier down on her."

"Yes - She'll be trapped for a while. Run while we still can - on to save Spoon Licker."

9

They ran as fast as their little troll legs would carry them, arriving at the Monster Worm's cave just before dawn. Since they were half-ogre, the sun would not turn them to rock, but it was better not to be seen. They crawled, then slunk, then tip-toed through the caves to find Spoon Licker. They found him quickly and carried him out of the cave before the Monster Worm found them.

"Stufur," Door slammer said, "go back and tell the others Gryla's on a rampage looking for all of us. Get them to meet at the place in Norway."

 "Alright, you take care of Spoon Licker and ask Skyr Gobbler to talk to the Hidden and see if they can find Door Sniffer." Stufur replied.

So, Spoon Licker and Door Slammer headed for Norway, to their favorite troll R&R spot, while Skyr Gobbler went to find Door Sniffer's trail, and Stufur headed back to the Yule Lad cave to collect his remaining eight brothers and flee the country.

Spoon Licker and Door Slammer caught two puffin and convinced them to fly to Tromsø, where human had wonderful spas built. The area nearby was perfect for troll relaxing too. There was a long history of Viking and Sámi settlements in the area and the Yule Lads had been there many times.

Meanwhile, Stufur burst into the Yule Lad cave, desperate to warn his brothers about Gryla's anger towards them.   The cave was in shambles. He stood in shock, looking around the terrible mess. Was he too late?

10

"YAY!" Stufur jumped, crashing his head into the low rock ceiling after Gully Gawk shouted in his ear.

The relief at seeing his brother-troll unharmed almost made Stufur want to hug him, or would, if he weren't a troll. "What happened?" Stufur asked.

"Sina came by and told us about Gryla and how you brought part of the glacier down on her. Har! That would have been fun to see. We're packing fast to, um, *relocate* for a while." His troll grin was more of a sneer.

"Good. We meet the others in Tromsø."

"You go ahead. Window Peeper, Candle Beggar and Sheep Cote Clod went to Kreative Dage in Denmark. Stir up a lil'troll trouble yes?" Stufur cackled.

"I'll go get them, but we might be a few days." Gully Gawk shouted over his shoulder as he ran out the cave entrance.

* * ** * *

Pot Scraper, Bowl Licker, Sausage Swiper and Meat Hook left with Stufur, sneaking a ride on a fishing trawler heading to Norway. It was a long four days for the fishermen.

"Argh, Troll Trouble." one shouted when he found the fish storage empty.

"Yow! Troll Trouble," groaned another when he found nets tangled in the winch.

The Yule Lads tampered with the sensors, the sonar, and the GPS. While the fishermen all worked on the problems, the Yule Lads were having a great meal in the food mess.

Sausage Swiper had both hands full and Pot Scraper had his head in a pan when they heard heavy boots clomping down the stairs. Yikes! They had to hide – quick.

11

Door Slammer loafed in Norway as Spoon Licker recovered from his encounter with the Monster Worm.

Within days of their arrival, spoons started disappearing from kitchens and restaurants. Door were caught by unexplained drafts, slamming shut with bone-jarring force. Thump-thump-thump…..tap-tap-tap. Door Slammer pounded on doors, knocked softly, and every now and then just blew the door back and forth to hear the hinges squeak and squawk.

Spoon Licker ran happily from house to house, grabbing spoons gobbled dough, batter and sauces.

"More troll trouble?" one cook groaned. "A few days ago it was sweet breads and cakes, now spoons gone missing?"

Spoon Licker stopped. They must be talking about Door Sniffer. He came by this way and they had to find him before he went back to Iceland and ran into Gryla.

Grabbing Door Slammer, they headed northeast, across Sweden. They stayed out of sight but snuck through all the kitchens in the best restaurants and inns. They found his trail and followed him clear to Finland.

"First the coffeecake and now the yogurt too." a sous chef moaned. Door Slammer knew Skyr Gobbler was with Door Sniffer.

They consulted trolls in Finland, who promised to send word to Stufur and the other four Yule Lads to meet them. They were getting closer. Door Slammer had a pretty good idea of the source of those amazing smells Door Sniffer was tracking.

If he was right, they were going to need all their troll power together in one place.

12

Gully Gawk peeked out from under the low table in Kronborg Castle with Sheep Cote Code beside him. Their mouths stretched wide in troll-like grins. Candle Beggar was in the shadows and Window Peeper was high on top of a cabinet. Sheep Cote Clod snickered at the confused lady looking for her car keys, which now hung from Window Peeper's bony fingers. The keyring's rhinestones glittered in the beams of sunshine and they clinked as Window Peeper moved, admiring them.

She heard the noise and started to look up. Quickly, Candle Beggar squawked from one side of the room. She whipped around to the direction of the noise.

Gully Gawk gave a horribly fake sneeze and the lady jumped in that direction. Sheep Cote gave a troll-moan and the lady jumped straight up in the air then ran for the door, muttering loudly.

"Oopha, we got troll trouble."

They had snuck across Denmark for days now, swiping milk, and pilfering shiny keepsakes, taste-testing and playing troll pranks. They had slinked and slithered from Amalienborg to Rundetarn. They never got tired of hearing someone groan, "Troll trouble."

They snickered at the frightened lady and they jumped from their hiding places. Hauling Window Peeper to the door, they peered out to see if the coast was clear.

A white and orange object was flung straight at them! Candle Beggar was hit straight on the head and knocked on his backside.

13

"Hey - What's this?" cried Window Peeper to the swooping, crashing Puffin.

"Come, come," it squawked. "Door Sniffer says meet in Finland. We have whale-ride ready for you."

"Whale? Sweeeet…." Howled Gully Gawk. "Let's go."

They followed the weaving puffin, who waddled into a fast run, desperately flapping its wings to awkwardly gain flight. Ducking from building to trees, the Yule Lads kept out of sight of humans, making their way to the coast.

They arrived at the Baltic Sea just as night fell and they waded out to the waiting whales. Window Peeper and Candle Beggar jumped on one, while Gully Gawk and Sheep Cote Clod scrambled atop the other. The whales took off across the Sea towards Finland, diving and jumping through the water, the Lads hanging on for the ride of their life.

"Whoo Hoo!"

The puffin flew off to deliver the same instructions to the group of Yule Lad trolls on the trawler once it docked in Norway. He flew fast and made it to the port to find the ship deserted and watched as the five stowaway Yule Lads snuck ashore.

"Stufur," he squawked, wings flapping wildly as he crashed in the troll's head.

"What the? Arrgggg, what does Door Slammer want now?" Stufur growled. "He always sends message by puffin."

"He says to go to Finland, that you would know where and why," the puffin said in his whistles and clicks.

"Hah!" Stufur replied, rolling his eyes with a fiendish smile. "Oh, Yes, I know. Our favorite kind of Troll Trouble." he shouted to his troll-brothers.

14

oor Sniffer's huge nose quivered as he took a deep breath. The smells were wonderful. There were cookies, of course, and sweet breads, cinnamon rolls and terta, pastries and pies and so much more! Troll slobber oozed out of his mouth and slowly globbed in huge drips, smearing on his shoulder, pooling by his knee as he crouched near the kitchen building. The compound was very busy and he had been waiting a long time for a chance to run across the courtyard.

Reindeer bellowed to each other and the trainers shouted as they worked with the newbies. The Big Guy's Southern Training camp was in a state of frenzied excitement this time of year. The Mrs. used the big kitchens here to try out new recipes and everyone wanted to taste test. Door Sniffer wanted to be a part of it, but he was definitely uninvited.

Skyr Gobbler kept him company until he found the stock of Viili, the Finnish yogurt that was a lot like Icelandic Skyr. Door Sniffer hadn't seen him since but heard a lot of yelling of "troll trouble" from the dairy buildings.

Now that Stufur, Pot Scraper and Spoon Licker were here, they would work together to get into that kitchen and get their hands on those treats! He shivered in excitement. He saw the signal and knew the ruckus was about to begin.

Ka-plow - Wham - Boom.   Rumbling sounds thundered across the small village. A small avalanche of snow slid off the barn roof and three figures jumped under the eaves of the stable. Sheep Cote Clod and Gully Gawk were after the milk.

Trolls converged on the kitchen - Door Sniffer ran in the back as everyone else ran out the front.
"EEEKKKKK!!!"

15

The Southern Reindeer Training Camp was in a state of pandemonium. A terrible racket rose from each building – reindeer bellowing, men shouting, women screeching, cows moo'ing, and the clatter of dishes falling and breaking.

The thirteen Yule Lads hadn't really meant to cause such a fuss. Gully Gawk and Sheep Cote Clod just snuck into the barn for a little milk. It was a total accident that Gully Gawk slipped off the beam he was walking and landed on the backside of a sleeping reindeer, who jumped up so suddenly she kicked the water bucket, which went flying into the wall, spraying water all over two cows, a horse and three other reindeer and a small flock of chickens. Truly, it was the chickens that raised such a fuss and then the whole barn was in a tizzy.

Stufur, Door Sniffer, Pot Scraper, Bowl Licker, Spoon Licker, Sausage Swiper and Meat Hook were all in the kitchen and couldn't be blamed for the ruckus outside. Inside was a different story. When everyone ran outside to see what was going on, Door Sniffer took advantage of the empty kitchen – and the other six Yule Lads were right behind him. Well, empty kitchen except the one girl that screamed and fell over faint at the sight of the Yule Lads.

They tore through the kitchen, snatching every sweet treat, spoon, pot, pan, and sausage link they could find, leaving behind a terrible mess. Grinning wickedly, they ran to the forest nearby and devoured the stolen goods. Their troll lips smacked together as they drooled and slobbered their way through the treats.

Pot Scraper spit out a mouthful when the forest around them exploded in shouts and snorts.

16

Stufur watched as Gully Gawk was tackled by three Elf Supervisors just on the other side of the bushes. Each of the elves were covered in chicken feathers and straw and looked like they had been in the barn when they ruckus took place. They didn't look happy about it either. "You come with us," Stufur heard one shout.

"The Reindeer Council will want to hear about this," said another, "you've thrown our training schedule completely out of whack. The camp's a mess and I'm not getting blamed for this."

Pot Scraper crawled over to a break in the bushes and squinted for a better look. The Elves were joined by a small herd of reindeer and they all surrounded Gully Gawk. Pot Scraper watched as they jumped on the reindeer, who quickly leapt into the air and few towards the north. Pot Scraper, Bowl Licker and the rest of the Yule Lads hiding in the trees looked at each other. They had to get to the Council to tell their side of the story before the elves did.

Bowl Licker sent a puffin ahead to make arrangements for all twelve Yule Lads to get ride across the ocean.

As quickly as they could, the troll brothers took off for the coast. When they arrived, they jumped on a polar bear transport and headed for the North Pole.

On the way, Stufur laid out the plan. "Sheep Cote, Door Slammer, Window Peeper and I will go see the Council," he said. "Spoon Licker, you take Pot Scraper, Bowl Licker and Door Sniffer and find where they're keeping Gully Gawk. Keep him company so nothing else happens. Everyone *behave*." He warned. "Candle Beggar, you and Meat Hook go with Sausage Swiper, and Skyr Gobbler. See if you can get any friends you have up there – elf or reindeer – to help us out."

Let's go get Gully Gawk.

17

The polar bears landed on the southern shore of the North Pole. All twelve Yule Lads scrambled off, waved their thanks, and then took off for the village.

"Stufur!" a happy elf with a crooked smile gave the troll a big hug. "I didn't think you'd be around here for a while after the troll trouble you caused last year."

"Um, yeah, well, that was an accident," Stufur mumbled, looking away and shuffling his feet. "I know Mrs. C probably hasn't forgiven us yet, but we had another little misunderstanding."

"Har-Har!" the elf laughed as he clapped Stufur on the back. "That's what I love about the Icelandic Yule Lads. Never a dull moment. How can the Council help?"

Stufur put his arm around the elf and whispered in his ear. Across the villages, groups of trolls pleaded their case with elves, reindeer and a variety of other magical creatures. As they finished, each couldn't resist the temptations around the village.

Sheep Cote Clod snuck into the barn for some milk. Skyr Gobbler crept into the dairy in search of yogurt while Sausage Swiper and Meat Hook tiptoed into the smokehouse.

Door Sniffer could not keep still. This was the source of the most wonderful kitchen smells in the world. When the wind was just right, he could smell the fresh baked goods all the way to Iceland. The cookies and sweetbreads, pies and cakes, even the thick fluffy frosting in the layered tertas smelled better than anywhere else.

He crept closer and looked in the window, globs of troll-drool dripping from the corners of his mouth. His huge nose twitched as he savored the scents of cinnamon, vanilla, nutmeg, and sugar. His toes tapped and his fingers curled. He was trying so hard to be good.

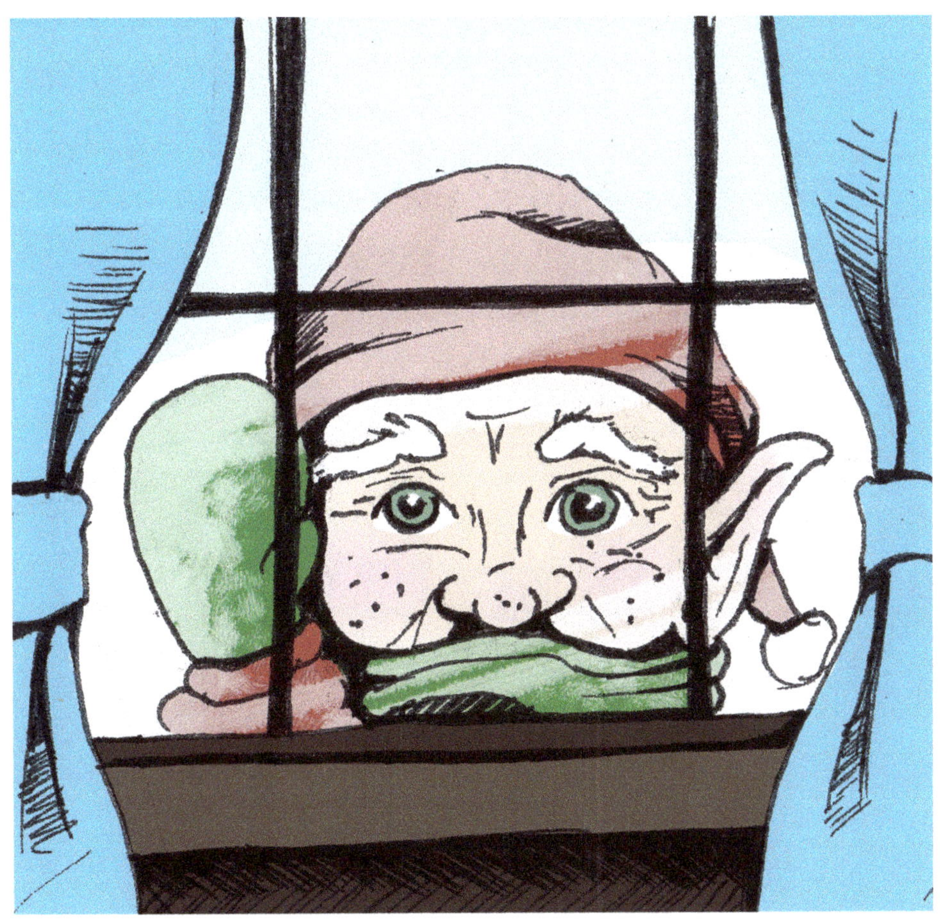

Spoon Licker joined him at the window, his eyes tracking every ooey-gooey spoon from tabletop to counter. Pot Scraper stood on his toes, eyeing the huge pile of pans waiting to be washed, whining a little as, like Door Sniffer, the troll-slobber and drool dripped from his mouth in anticipation.

"GGGGRRRRR" a ferocious growl followed by a furious barking broke the silence.

18

B owl Licker had tried to snatch the bowl from Rufus. The huge North Pole sheepdog had latched on the edge with his teeth as Bowl Licker pulled with both hands. Door Sniffer fell over laughing when he saw Bowl Licker brace his feet against the sheepdog's chest. Rufus refused to let go of the bowl. He shook his mighty head back and forth and poor Bowl Licker flapped around like a wet rag.

The sound of running footsteps in the hall sent them all through the closest doorway. Door Sniffer, Spoon Licker, Pot Scraper and Bowl Licker scrambled around the dim room, each finding a small hiding place. Bowl Licker ducked behind the door. Door Sniffer jumped in a large open barrel. Pot Scraper scrambled up the shelves with Spoon Licker hot on his heels. They each found canisters and boxes to hide behind. This was some closet. They listened for a moment to the sounds coming from the kitchen. It was calming down so they felt a bit braver. The small dim room smelled wonderful.

Door Sniffer popped his head up and reached over to a nearby shelf. Cookies! He nibbled on a few. Getting more daring, he crawled out of the barrel and up to the next shelf. It was lined with fruit-filled cakes. He nibbled some more. Spoon Licker started exploring too. There weren't any ooey-gooey spoons in there, but he saw a canister of clean ones waiting to be needed. He needed one. Carefully, he crawled over to snatch one as Pot Scraper explored the shelf below. Bowl Licker was on the other side of the room, watching his three troll brothers crawl around, sniffing, slurping, and drooling over everything.

He heard a creaking sound. He heard a crack.

The wood shelves started to moan and groan and Bowl Licker saw the whole wall come crashing towards him. Flour flew in the air, sugar sprayed everywhere and there was a choking thick cloud of cinnamon that rose in a puff of smoke. Corn syrup oozed from jars and dripped, joining with globs of honey and strawberry preserves to make a huge sticky mess in the center of the floor.

The four Yule Lads were buried!

19

"Quick – go – go –go" Bowl Licker shouted after he swallowed the glob of honey-flour-nutmeg mixture that had filled his mouth.

"Phew-ack." Spoon Licker hacked as he coughed up a cloud of powdered sugar and cinnamon. He slipped as he tried to stand and slid toward the door.

Door Sniffer raised his head, covered in four and gooey corn syrup. He tried to wipe the stickiness from his nose and just added to the mess when he smeared the raspberry preserves from his hands to his face. As he stood, he leaned on the wall, leaving behind grimy handprints.

Bowl Licker grabbed Pot Scraper and pulled him along to the door. The room behind them was in shambles. They didn't look back and they moved as fast as their troll legs would go toward the back door of the kitchen. They had just reached the outdoors when they heard the chaos from the kitchen.

"Yikes - all the cookies and cakes are destroyed."

"What a mess – look at the piles of gook. And there's flour on *everything*."

"Look - Troll handprints and troll footprints."

"Agh! We got troll trouble."

"Mrs. C is gonna cry when she sees her kitchen."

Pot Scraper and his three troll brothers ran for the closest barn. They found Sheep Cote Clod and quickly explained their new mischief.

"Yikes - we've got to get out of here," he shouted, "Go get the rest of our troll brothers and get back to the cave. I'll get Gully Gawk."

They flew through the North Pole compound, barely avoiding the elves, reindeer and other creatures tracking their very obvious sticky and gooey footprints. Very quickly, all thirteen had been gathered and took off towards Iceland. Suddenly, dealing with Gryla didn't sound too bad. They were all afraid of what would happen if they stayed here.

20

"Santa, we got troll trouble!" Mrs. Claus stood with her hands on her hips, fifteen elves, four reindeer, three sprites, two reindeer trainers, and eight fairies stood behind her.

They all began speaking at once. "The cookies are gone."

"The reindeer barn is a mess of hay mixed with the straw and milk dumped everywhere."

"There's no Skyr for the morning oatmeal."

"It will take days to clean up the mess in the kitchen."

Santa held up both hands in defense, "ho – ho – ho." He shook his head laughing, "One at a time please."

"You there, what seems to be the problem?" he said to a little sprite.

"Santa, you have to do something. These Yule Lads come up here and run around causing trouble and we always have to spend days cleaning up the mess."

"Hmm," said Santa, "Well, now OK. I see that would be quite upsetting, yes."

"Mrs. Claus, what do you think?"

"Santa, they are so active and they act without thinking and turn everything upside down. And I don't know if we have enough time this year to replace all the cookies they just ruined. I just don't know if we can welcome them here in the future." She shook her head, sad because she like them but they really did cause such a mess.

"I like those guys, all thirteen." Santa said, pacing as he continued, "They were raised to be very bad, well their mother was an ogre-troll after all. But, now they do *try* not to be bad. It's really not their fault they really don't know how to be good."

He stopped suddenly, "But a year with no cookies? I don't know, I don't know. They should learn a lesson. We should send a puffin message that they cannot come for a visit for at least six months."

An elf jumped up and ran to Santa. Standing on his tip-toes as Santa leaned down, the elf whispered urgently into his ear.

Santa smiled, "Yes, yes, that is an excellent idea. Everyone. No toys or gifts for the Icelandic Yule Lads this year."

The elves, reindeer, sprites, fairies and Mrs. Claus all gasped.

"Surely, you don't mean it," Mrs. Claus sputtered, "You have never made such a decision so far before Christmas. Are you sure?"

"Yes, I'm sorry. I have no choice but to move the Yule Lads to the Naughty List."

21

Back in the Yule Lad cave in Iceland, Window Peeper read the news on his puffin-pad. It was the usual troll-squabbles, near-sightings with humans then he saw it. A Special News bulletin….. he still couldn't believe it. Santa had sent the email yesterday and now the rest of the world knew.

The Icelandic Yule Lads are in an uproar today as shocking news comes in from the North Pole. It is said that the communication comes directly from the big guy, Santa, himself. Sources report that Window Peeper, the social media representative of the Yule Lads, was literally knocked over with a puffin feather after reading Santa's message. In a ground-breaking decision, Santa has notified that the Yule Lads, all 13, have been banned from the annual Nice List. It is not clear whether the decision is for this year only or is a permanent status for the Lads.

While details are still sketchy, reports from sources at the North Pole indicate that Santa has lost patience with the Yule Lad's antics and mischief-making. Between Pot Licker, Spoon Licker, and Stufur, Mrs. Claus wasn't able to serve a decent meal until March last year. This year's ruckus seems to have started at the Southern Reindeer training camp and before the Reindeer Council could meet, the Yule Lads showed up at the North Pole.

Sources say all thirteen Yule Lads were involved in one of four separate incidents around the village. There was the disappearance of a large number of sausages and meats from the smokehouse, most of the yogurt was eaten, the milk was completely drained dry, and the entire stock of candles has gone missing. The final straw, it seems, was the destruction the kitchen storage room and many of the cookies and cakes that had been prepared for the upcoming holiday season. Mrs. Clause is doubtful that the holiday cookie stores can be replenished in time. Rumor has it the reindeer threatening to boycott deliveries this year so Santa felt he had no choice but to take this extreme action.

"Window Peeper, are you sure that's what it says?" demanded Door Slammer.

"Why would Santa do that?" cried Sausage Swiper.

"It's not fair," Bowl Licker sobbed.

All thirteen Yule Lads sat in their cold Icelandic cave. They usually loved the holiday season but this year was different.

As young trolls, their mother, Gryla had taught them to be bad. In time, they learned on their own to be less bad, and definitely not evil anymore. They were sort of naughty but kind of nice. They did leave gifts in the shoes of children in whose homes they caused mischief.

"Why would he decide we were naughty?" wondered Stufur, "we didn't mean to do anything bad on purpose, it was all accidents."

"Well, it does happen a lot I guess," Window Peeper said. "Maybe they wouldn't have been so upset if we cleaned up some of the mess."

"Do you think maybe doing something nice would help?" asked Bowl Licker.

"I don't know. Maybe we've been selfish. We like to take treats and I guess we do make a mess and cause trouble." Spoon Licker said.

"Do you think being selfish and never doing anything nice for anyone else is why Santa thinks we're naughty?" Skyr Gobbler looked at his troll brothers.

* * * * *

They had never thought of it before. Naughty was doing something bad on purpose, wasn't it? Could it be that never thinking of anyone but yourself was also naughty?

They thought of their North Pole friends and the ones at the Southern
Reindeer Training Camp. They had caused a lot of extra work for their friends and
had never told them they were sorry. Each of the Yule Lads though of the reindeer,
elves, sprites and other friends they had and missed them. They were all silent, each
thinking private thoughts.

One by one, they left the cave. They each went in separate directions, intent
on their own private errands.

22

Far away at the North Pole, Santa smiled as he watched through his magical glasses. He watched the Yule Lads snuck into the barns and kitchens and all those places they had made a mess. Using their troll magic, they each tried to do something nice for those who ended up with the extra work from the Yule Lad's antics.

Sheep Cote Clod replaced the sheep's milk and fed all the sheep

Gully Gawk replaced the cow's milk and cleaned all the pens.

Stufur used his troll magic to replace all the cookies and sweets at the North Pole, then scrubbed away all the troll slobber from the windows and walls.

Spoon Licker left a dozen new spoons in Mrs. C's kitchen and mopped all the floors.

Pot Licker washed all the dishes at the North Pole, the Reindeer Camp, and several town in Finland.

Bowl Licker took three new toys and a big bone to Rufus then took treats to all his puffin and whale friends.

Door Slammer oiled all the squeaky hinges at the North Pole and throughout all of Sweden and didn't slam a single door while he was there.

Skyr Gobbler replaced all the Skyr at the North Pole and in Iceland.

Sausage Swiper restocked the Southern Reindeer smokehouse then cleaned out every chimney in Norway he could find.

Window Peeper returned the sparkly keys he had swiped and cleaned all the windows in Denmark.

Door Sniffer used his troll magic to fix all the shelves in Mrs. C's pantry.

Meat Hook left a holiday roast at the home of every elf and stocked up Mrs C's freezer with burgers and hot dogs.

Candle Beggar left big piles of scented candles at the North Pole, the Reindeer Training Camp and one in every home in Iceland.

Santa was pleased they had realized how selfish they had been. This year, they learned to be considerate of other people's feelings. The North Pole and the Southern Reindeer Training Camp were filled with happiness. The helpful work and gifts from the Yule Lads were appreciated but no one knew who to thank. Not a single Yule Lad had left a note nor told anyone what they had done.

Santa's eyes twinkled as he wrote an email to the Yule Lads and then updated the Naughty & Nice lists.

As Window Peeper read the note from Santa aloud to the rest of his troll brothers, they were all silent. None of them had told anyone what they had done. They were trolls after all, and not expected to do nice things. They looked at each other nervously. "I think this was a good thing," said Stufur carefully, "we can be trolls and still do nice things sometimes."

"Yes," said Door Slammer with a troll-grin, "especially if no one can prove it was us!"

With a whoop, all thirteen trolls began to dance around and celebrate. They were back on Santa's Nice List and would soon be in the homes and villages of Iceland to enjoy their favorite time of year.

Every year, The Yule Lads come down from the Icelandic mountains each day starting on December 12th. They travel one by one, until they are all together for Christmas Eve. Then, after Christmas, they leave to return to their mountain home, one by one each day in the order they arrived.

December 12: Stekkjastaur (Stek ja' stir) Sheep Cote Clod
December 13: Giljagaur (Gil ya gur) Gully Gawk
December 14: Stúfur (Stew fur) Stubby
December 15: Þvörusleikir (Thur-a slaker) Spoon Licker
December 16: Pottaskefill (Pot-a skae fill) Pot Scraper
December 17: Askasleikir (Aska slaker) Bowl Licker
December 18: Hurðaskellir (Hurtha Sketler) Door Slammer
December 19: Skyrgámur (Skeyr-gow mur) Skyr Gobbler
December 20: Bjúgnakrækir (Buke naw cry gear) Sausage Swiper
December 21: Gluggagægir (Glugga-guy year) Window Peeper
December 22: Gáttaþefur (Gotta thever) Door Sniffer
December 23: Ketkrókur (Ket croaker) Meat Hook
December 24: Kertasnikir (Keta sneaker) Candle Beggar